Claire Llewellyn

Snakes

Illustrated by Steve Roberts

OXFORD
UNIVERSITY PRESS

This book belongs to

OXFORD
UNIVERSITY PRESS

Great Clarendon Street, Oxford OX2 6DP

Oxford University Press is a department of the University of Oxford.
It furthers the University's objective of excellence in research, scholarship,
and education by publishing worldwide in

Oxford New York

Athens Auckland Bangkok Bogotá Buenos Aires Calcutta
Cape Town Chennai Dar es Salaam Delhi Florence Hong Kong Istanbul
Karachi Kuala Lumpur Madrid Melbourne Mexico City Mumbai
Nairobi Paris São Paulo Singapore Taipei Tokyo Toronto Warsaw

with associated companies in Berlin Ibadan

Oxford is a registered trade mark of Oxford University Press
in the UK and in certain other countries

Text copyright © Claire Llewellyn 2000
Illustrations copyright © Steve Roberts 2000

Hardback ISBN 0–19–910614-2
Paperback ISBN 0–19–910615-0
Pack of 6 ISBN 0-19-910757-2
Pack of 36 ISBN 0-19-910758-0

This edition is also available in Oxford Reading Tree
Branch Library Stages 8-10 Pack A

1 3 5 7 9 10 8 6 4 2

Printed and bound in Portugal by Edições ASA

Contents

▶ Looking at snakes   4

▶ A world of snakes   8

▶ A snake's scales   10

▶ What do snakes eat?   13

▶ What makes a good hunter?   15

▶ Death by squeezing   18

▶ Death by poison   20

▶ Dinner time   24

▶ Egg-eating snakes   26

▶ Snake attacks   28

▶ Glossary   30

▶ Looking at snakes

Snakes are curious creatures.

They have no ears. They have no legs or feet. They have a long, smooth, scaly body. They have glassy eyes that never close and a tongue that flicks in and out.

Indian cobra

Green tree python

Adders

Snakes **slither** and **wriggle** and **twist** and turn. They seem to flow along the ground like water.

Blunt-nosed snake

5

There are at least 3000 kinds of snakes in the world. And there may well be many more.

A few of these snakes are real giants. An anaconda's body is thicker than your waist. And there are pythons as long as a bus.

Green anaconda

But most kinds of snake are much smaller than this. In fact, a few of them are more like worms.

A Thread snake is as thin as the lead in a pencil. It's the smallest snake in the world.

Thread snake

▶ A world of snakes

Snakes live all over the world.

The Tiger snake lives in the hot, dusty lands of Australia.

The Elephant trunk snake lives in rivers and the salty sea.

The Bushmaster lives in the rainforests of South America.

Rattlesnakes live in the deserts of North America.

On hot days, rattlesnakes hide from the sun. They curl up and sleep in an old, dead cactus or a burrow under the ground. At dusk they wake up, uncurl themselves, and slither out into the night.

Western diamond-back rattlesnake

Did you know...
Rattlesnakes get their name from the rings on their tail, which they rattle when danger is near.

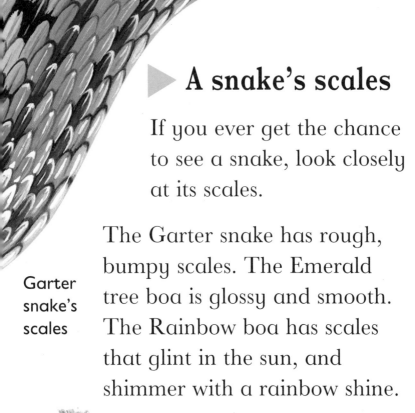

► A snake's scales

If you ever get the chance to see a snake, look closely at its scales.

Garter snake's scales

The Garter snake has rough, bumpy scales. The Emerald tree boa is glossy and smooth. The Rainbow boa has scales that glint in the sun, and shimmer with a rainbow shine.

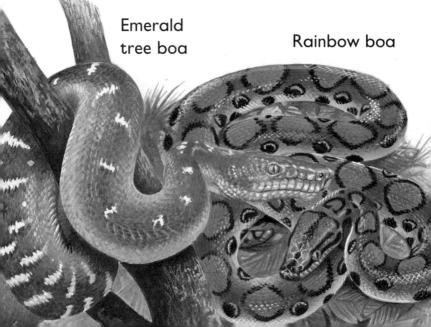

Emerald tree boa

Rainbow boa

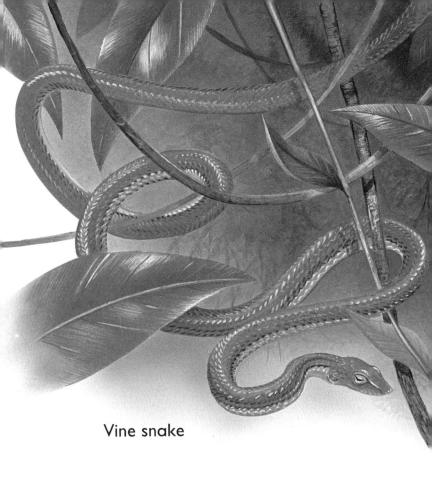

Vine snake

Many kinds of snake are hard to
see because the colour of their
scales helps to hide them.

A Vine snake looks like a creeper.

A Bushmaster looks like a pile of
dead leaves.

Eyelash viper

An Eyelash viper hides among the fruit of a tree.

An Orange sand viper hides under the sand.

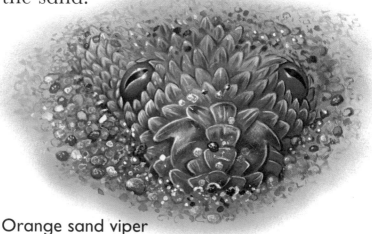

Orange sand viper

▶ What do snakes eat?

Snakes have to eat to stay alive and not one of them is vegetarian.

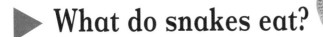

Small snakes, like Thread snakes, eat snails, grubs and flies.

Medium snakes, like rattlesnakes, eat birds, mice and frogs.

Timber
rattlesnake

African rock python

And big snakes, like pythons, eat wild pigs and deer. Some will even tackle a crocodile.

Snakes have to catch every meal they eat. They have to be very good hunters.

What makes a good hunter?

Many animals are good hunters.

A good hunter sees, hears or smells its prey, often from a long way away. A good hunter is quiet and sneaky and keeps out of sight of its prey.

A good hunter is fast and strong. It has weapons, such as teeth or claws. And it kills its prey quickly before it can fight back or get away.

Grass snake

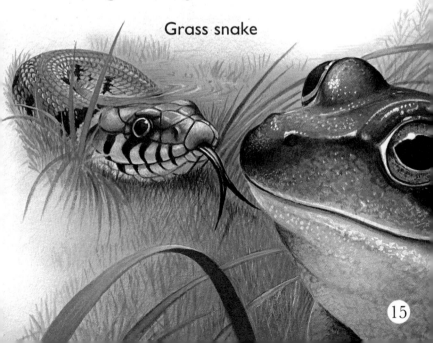

Snakes are silent hunters.
They make no footsteps
because they have no feet.
They grip the ground with
their scales, and their muscles
pull their bodies into bends.

Fer-de-lance

Vine snake

In forests, they glide up the trunks of the trees. Then they slip among the leaves and wind their tails around a branch, and do what snakes do best ... they keep very still and wait.

Boa constrictor

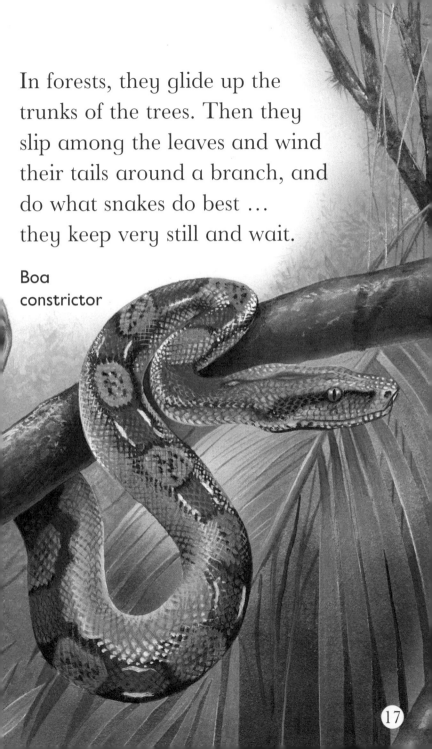

▶ Death by squeezing

Many of the biggest snakes kill by squeezing.

A Boa constrictor hides in the trees. As soon as an animal passes underneath, the snake drops down and winds around its prey. The animal struggles and tries to get free. But each time it breathes out, the snake squeezes **tighter**... and **tighter**... and **tighter**.

Boa constrictor

Soon the animal can no longer breathe. Soon the animal is dead.

Gaboon viper

▶ Death by poison

Some kinds of snake don't fight their prey. They kill it with poison instead. The poison is made inside their cheeks, and squirts out through their sharp, hollow fangs.

Vipers are poisonous.
Like many snakes, they are out and about at night. They cannot see their prey in the dark like a cat. They cannot hear it like an owl.

But they can taste it in the air with their flicking, forked tongue and silently track it down.

Puff adder

21

Some vipers have a special trick.
It's almost like seeing in the dark.

On the front of their head
they have two little holes which
feel the heat of animals nearby.
A warm, living mouse makes
a mouse-shaped target. A warm,
living deer makes a deer-shaped
target. They stand out against
the cool night air.

The snake strikes the target
with its long, sharp fangs and
injects it with deadly poison.
Then the snake slips away
to hide somewhere safe.

It has to wait for its prey to die.

Pit viper

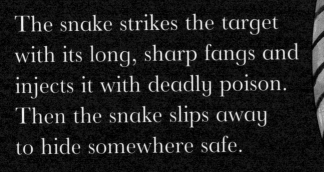

▶ Dinner time

A snake can take hours
to eat its dinner.
It doesn't gobble or tear
its food, or chew it up
bit by bit. It eats the
animal WHOLE!

Hog-nose snake

A snake can swallow animals bigger
than itself. Its skull bones come apart
to make lots of room. And its skin
is stretchy like elastic.

The snake **stretches**
its mouth over the animal's head.
Then it pulls in the body with its
jaws and teeth – first the left side
of the jaw, and then the right. It's
like pulling in a rope, one hand
over the other.

After a big meal
a snake feels
sleepy and hides
itself safely away.
The food leaves a
tell-tale lump in its
body and can take
days to disappear.

Did you know...
Pythons can survive on one meal a year,
if they eat something big like a zebra.

Egg-eating snake

▶ Egg-eating snakes

Some kinds of snake eat nothing
but eggs. But eggs can make
tricky meals.

The Egg-eating snake from Africa
swallows eggs three times bigger
than its head. (That's like you or
me swallowing a pumpkin!)

The snake has no teeth to crush
the shell. So it stretches its jaws
over the egg and "walks" it down
into its throat. The shell breaks
on a row of little spines. The hungry
snake swallows the slippery egg,
but spits out the hard bits of shell.

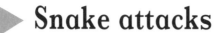

▶ Snake attacks

Snakes are shy animals. They like to keep themselves to themselves.

And yet they kill 30 000 people every year. Why is the number so high?

Snakes never eat people. They don't attack us because they are hungry. They attack us because they are very frightened, or mistake us for their usual prey.

Russell's viper

Most attacks happen in the parts of the world where snakes and people live side by side. People in these places often walk barefoot. And hospitals are far away. So here's some advice if you're on an expedition to a desert or a steamy rainforest.

- Always wear long trousers, and thick socks and boots.
- Never climb trees that have very thick leaves.
- Never swim in muddy rivers.
- Stand very still if you meet a snake.
- Don't go near it or try to touch it.
- If you are bitten on your arm or leg, try very hard not to move it. Never suck or cut out the poison. Cover the bite with a clean cloth and put it in a simple splint. Then find a doctor straightaway.

  And try not to worry: you are not about to die. Most poison takes many hours to work.

Glossary

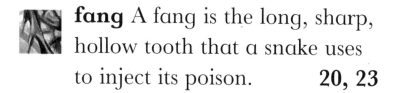

fang A fang is the long, sharp, hollow tooth that a snake uses to inject its poison. **20, 23**

poison Poison is the deadly juice made by some snakes when they bite. **20, 23, 29**

prey The animals that are hunted and killed by another animal for food are called prey. **15, 18, 20, 21, 23, 28**

rainforest A rainforest is a thick forest that grows in the warmest, wettest parts of the world. **8, 29**

scales Scales are the flat pieces that completely cover a snake's body. **10, 11, 16**

scaly Something that is covered with scales is scaly. **4**

 splint A splint is a piece of wood or metal that you tie to an injured part of the body to protect it and keep it still. **29**

 strike When a snake strikes, it suddenly attacks or bites. **23**

Reading Together

Oxford Reds have been written by leading children's authors who have a passion for particular non-fiction subjects. So as well as up-to-date information, fascinating facts and stunning pictures, these books provide powerful writing which draws the reader into the text.

Oxford Reds are written in simple language, checked by educational advisors. There is plenty of repetition of words and phrases, and all technical words are explained. They are an ideal vehicle for helping your child develop a love of reading – by building fluency, confidence and enjoyment.

You can help your child by reading the first few pages out loud, then encourage him or her to continue alone. You could share the reading by taking turns to read a page or two. Or you could read the whole book aloud, so your child knows it well before tackling it alone.

Oxford Reds will help your child develop a love of reading and a lasting curiosity about the world we live in.

Sue Palmer
Writer and Literacy Consultant